What They're Say...

'Disappearing Diamonds ... readers.' *The West Roxbury* ...

'The beginning, middle an... this a good story with educ... perfect for school-aged kids.' *Kids First!*

'Move over McGruff the Crime Dog, Upton Charles is here to sniff for clues and solve your mysteries.' *Cantabrigia*

'One of its appealing aspects is that it is a mystery, the other is that the main character is a dog detective who thinks out loud as the narrator of the story. Note, he is not a talking dog, just a dog whose thoughts we can hear.' *Kids First!*

'This dog takes a bite out of crime.' *Cambridge Chronicle*

'Perfect for the read-to-me or the I-can-read-it myself age group.' *Boston Globe*

'D. G. Stern's delightful series of adventures starring Upton Charles.' *Flipkart.com*

'Upton Charles will make a believer out of every reader.' *Midwest Book Review*

'To solve the paw-fect crime, call Upton!' *The Harvard Coop*

'Told from the viewpoint of a very special dog, "Winter Wonderland" promises to be a great mystery reading experience for kids ages 8-11. "Winter Wonderland" also can be read aloud by an adult as an exciting chapter book for a younger audience.' *Midwest Book Review*

'This story is entertaining and educational with historical facts and valuable social lesson to be learned. The message inherent in the story is that things do not always have to be worth a lot of money to be valuable.' *Kids First!*

'The action-packed mysteries are intended to be "read with me" books so that parents and teachers can be involved with reading at an earlier age. Older readers can also read through and enjoy them on their own.' *NewportPatch*

'Logical deductive thinking, teamwork, paying attention to random clues to put the jigsaw puzzle together, who would think these skills could be helped and taught by a dog, even a very smart dog?' *Entrepreneur.com*

'As a teacher of constructive logical, deductive thought, Upton rules.' *Midwest Book Review*

'Upton Charles is a positive character, the family members are appealing and the story is engaging. The illustrations are quite simple and the story's historical facts give it extra depth.' *Kids First!*

'The adorable, astute Upton is full of energy and humorous "remarks" as he tries to communicate with humans. This is sure to be a favorite with most all children!' *Rockin' Book Reviews*

UPTON CHARLES

Dog Detective

Tip Top

By D.G. Stern

Illustrations by Deborah Allison

NEPTUNE PRESS

WWW.NEPTUNEPRESS.ORG

NEPTUNE PRESS

WWW.UPTONCHARLES.COM

Printed in the U.S.A.

Publisher's Cataloging-In-Publication Data
Stern, D. G.
   Upton Charles, dog detective. Tip top / by D.G. Stern ; illustrations by Deborah Allison.

     pages : illustrations ; cm

   Summary: "The carnival is in town and the twins really want to go. Upton is not too keen on the idea until the Chief of Police calls and says that there has been a disappearance--the snake lady and all her snakes are gone. Upton, who is a Bichon Frise, a little white dog, knows his duty and joins the Charles' to sniff out the missing reptiles, although he has no idea what a snake smells like."--Provided by publisher.
   Interest age level: 008-011.
   ISBN: 978-0-9906103-2-8

   1. Dogs--Juvenile fiction. 2. Bichon frise--Juvenile fiction. 3. Snakes--Juvenile fiction. 4. Lost articles--Juvenile fiction. 5. Missing persons--Juvenile fiction. 6. Dogs--Fiction. 7. Snakes--Fiction. 8. Lost and found possessions--Fiction. 9. Missing persons--Juvenile fiction. 10. Mystery and detective stories. 11. Mystery fiction. I. Allison, Deborah, 1967- II. Title. III. Title: Tip top

PZ7.S74 Upt 2015
[Fic]   2015900493

"Life is like a carnival ride, it has its ups, its downs, and all its twerks. But we all know that in the end it was fun and worth the wild ride"

– Terrin White

CHAPTER ONE
Nap Time is Over

I've got to try and run...faster...faster. I've got to get away before... All I have time for is a quick glance behind me. It's gaining. I can see the massive head with bared fangs lunging at me. I can't move any faster. Be smart...find a hiding place. Be deceptive...throw him off your trail. No time. There's no time. It's too late.

"Upton.Upton," a voice calls to me. "Wake up. You're having a bad dream." A hand starts to gently shake me into consciousness. I open up one eye, then the other. Whoa! That was a really bad dream. It seemed so real. I slowly turn my head and see Mom bending over me–smiling.

"Are you okay?" she asks. I am now.

"Hey Mom," shout the twins, as they walk or rather, clump, clump, clump into the living room, where I've been napping on the couch. "What's wrong with Upton?"

"Nothing at all, kids. He had a nightmare, but he's fine now. Aren't you?"

I am now, and thank goodness Mom woke me up before I became a snack. I don't remember why that vicious dog was chasing me, but I thought I was dead meat–literally. What did I do to have angered a crazy canine enough to take a bite out of me? Nothing, I'm sure. I couldn't possibly have done anything to get that kind of reaction. I'm easy to get along with, friendly and generally pleasant. Everyone likes me...well, almost everyone.

"Veronica...Alex," Mom calls to the twins, "maybe Upton wants to go out. This would be a great time, since we've got a few minutes before dinner."

"How many minutes? I'm starving," Veronica whines.

"About a half hour," Mom replies.

"Will Dad be home?" Veronica asks.

"He's on his way. No problem."

"Awesome. We want to show him something we found online," continues Veronica.

"Yeah, but I found it," Alex tries to assert himself.

"Well, so what? I noticed how cool it was."

"Yo! Stop bickering and take Upton for a walk. Now!"

Sounds like a splendid idea to me. Since I'm not really supposed to be on the couch in the first place. Maybe if I quickly sneak off and find my leash, Mom won't get on my case. Maybe. Quick like a bunny, I leap to the floor and dash off into the kitchen, where my leash hangs from a hook that Dad installed after countless times when he couldn't figure out where the twins had put it.

Oh, by the way. My name is Upton...Upton Charles. I'm a Bichon Frise (that's "BEE-shon free-ZEY"), a little fluffy, very cute, white dog with big black eyes. I live with Mom, Dad, and the twins: Alex and Veronica. They're called fraternal twins because one is a girl and one is a boy and they are eleven years old...each. We live in a big house near the beach. Oh, I forgot, Watson. She's a cat and has been with us for about two months now. We adopted her after she decided to become my assistant detective. That's why I named her Watson–like Sherlock Holmes. The twins can't agree on a name for Watson, which doesn't seem to bother her. She's actually pretty cool for a c-a-t. She doesn't eat my food, doesn't need to go out for walks and basically hangs out.

But enough of that. I've got to go out for a walk in a big way, and do some doggie things. It would be in bad form to have an accident, especially since I just turned three.

CHAPTER TWO
Exceptional Dinner

"Dinner! Everyone wash up," Mom proclaims, as we return from a very pleasant stroll through the neighborhood. Sometimes walking with the twins is an adventure. Like, they 'forget' to stop at intersections–more often than not. On several occasions we've had some near misses–screeching tires and honking horns. Very frightening stuff, especially if you're connected to them by a leash with nowhere to go. However, since I am better trained than they are, I always stop at each corner, sit, and look both ways to see if there's a car coming. Even on one-way streets. I remember one time, even though there were no cars driving down the street, we were still almost hit by someone on a bicycle, riding the wrong way on a one-way street. One can never be too careful.

In any event, our walk is very enjoyable. The twins are calm and attentive. I wonder what they're scheming. I know that's not a nice thing to say, but whenever Alex and Veronica are quiet, they are usually thinking, and that in itself is scary. The ideas they come up with. Anyway, whatever it is that Mom has prepared smells great. Ahhh, boneless breast of chicken with tarragon, asparagus, and wild rice.

What! You think that dogs don't pay attention to what people eat? You are sadly mistaken. Despite being only three years old, I think I have developed a very sophisticated palate. Although I can discern quality food, I still tend to eat way too fast. I wonder if that's some sort of primal instinct that we canines still retain—eat fast, or someone else will eat your food. Obviously, that's not likely in our household. Well, except when Phoebe comes over to visit. Phoebe is my best friend. She lives around the corner from our house, and we get to play together a lot. Phoebe's a little older than I am—about six months, and substantially...how can I say this politely... heavier. Basically, Phoebe is a hog whenever there's food around. If there is any food left in my bowl (unlikely) or Watson's bowl, Phoebe will devour the contents. Sometimes Mom fills two doggie bowls and places them down on the floor for us. Not only will Phoebe eats hers, but before I've taken even four bites, she will be pushing me aside to eat my food as well. I let her, although for her own good, I should probably become more assertive. Oh, Phoebe is also a Bichon Frise, a very large Bichon Frise.

"Hi everyone," Dad says, entering the kitchen. He's certainly in a good mood.

"You sound very chipper," Mom comments.

"I had a great meeting. I think that the proposal went splendidly, and we've already been engaged to help with the preliminary planning."

"Congratulations." Mom gives him a big kiss, followed by high fives from the twins. Hello! I'll give him a kiss too–a doggie kiss, but that's not a cool guy thing to do, so I sit down and raise my paw. Watson joins me. Yip! Meow!

Bending down to take my extended paw, Dad says, "Thank you, Upton. Maybe this calls for some kind of special treat...later." He smiles, scratches Watson behind the ear, and walks to the sink, to wash up.

"First things first," Mom announces. "Dinner."

Sounds good to me. I love chicken, but unless it's boneless, I don't get any. Chicken bones can be very dangerous for a dog. Not so for a cat. They are very polite eaters. I could choke, or the bone could splinter if I chew it. I'd love to figure out a way to eat buffalo wings. They always smell so good; and to a dog, smell is important. Why be dissatisfied when what you are being offered is fabulous? Remember...eat slowly. Savor each bite.

CHAPTER THREE
The Carnival is in Town

I sort of take my time; but even so, I seem to have eaten my dinner substantially more quickly than the rest of the family. Maybe it's because I don't get to sit at the table and engage in meaningful conversation. Nevertheless, dinner was a huge success, especially if measured by the amount of leftovers, like none.

"Veronica, Alex, would you please clear our plates, in addition to yours?" Mom asks.

With a little more hesitation than

necessary, Alex and Veronica slowly remove the plates, silverware, empty platter, and glasses in front of Mom and Dad.

After what seems like an eternity, Dad announces, "Now that the table has been cleared, I'll put everything in the dishwasher and maybe we can all go out and get that special treat I mentioned. Any suggestions?"

"How about cotton candy?" the twins declare in unison. Cotton candy? Where in the world can you get cotton candy around here? I keep pretty good track of all the shops that sell delicious things to eat, and I've never seen one that offers cotton candy.

Obviously, Mom and Dad feel the same as I do. "Cotton candy?" they reply. "Is there a new store in town that sells cotton candy?"

"At the carnival," Alex and Veronica announce, jumping up and down.

"It opens tonight," Alex adds.

"At the park," Veronica chimes in. "It's here all the way until Sunday."

"Can we go?" they squeal.

Mom and Dad turn and face each other. I have a sense that going to the carnival with the twins is not exactly what they had in mind. Me neither. A little ice cream perhaps, or maybe even a piece of fudge, but a whole carnival, that's quite a different kettle of fish.

"What about tomorrow? It's Saturday and you don't have anything planned, except cleaning up your room," Mom announces.

"Because...because," Veronica sputters,

"like, everybody is going to be there tonight. All our friends and everything."

"If we go tonight, then I don't want to hear about going tomorrow or Sunday. Deal?" Dad negotiates.

"Why can't we go with our friends tomorrow?" Alex demands. "We're old enough."

"For one thing, you're not old enough to go to a traveling carnival alone, even during the day with all your friends," Mom begins. "And secondly, carnivals are very expensive. You have a choice...tonight with us, or tomorrow with... Dad."

Dad stares at Mom, raising one eyebrow higher than the other.

Mom shrugs and says, "I've got several appointments tomorrow. Sorry."

"But..." Alex starts.

"I don't want any ands, ifs, or buts, young man. Take it or leave it," Dad announces. "Anyway, tonight is my treat. Maybe Mom and I can take a few rides on the merry-go-round."

"What about the 'Hammer' or the 'Tilt-World'?" Veronica is obviously teasing–sort of.

"I said I would take you and pay. I never said that I would go on the rides," responds Dad.

"Twins, basically your father is a chicken. He hates rides. I guess they scare him. I'll ride the 'Hammer'." Mom grins at Dad.

"Fine with me."

This is all fine and good, but what am I supposed to do on a Friday evening if you all take off for the carnival? Watch TV with Watson. Not.

I would have been included on a trip to get an ice cream or fudge, but I'm not sure a little white dog is particularly welcome at a carnival. Well, if Dad doesn't go on any rides, maybe I can stay with him. It's only fair, after all. I wonder if they have any lions or tigers or other scary creatures at the carnival? I remember hearing once about a snake lady. She'd wrap herself with snakes and walk around. Ugh!

Meow! Watson just turns and walks away. Maybe it was because I mentioned lions and tigers.

"Can we call Sam to make sure he's going tonight?" Alex inserts.

"I thought simply everyone was going to be there." Dad smiles.

The twins look down at their feet. "He hasn't told his parents yet."

Mom and Dad burst out laughing. Hey! What about me? Yip!

CHAPTER FOUR
Now or Later

To go or not to go...that is the question. And one which I wish would be decided sooner rather than later. I'm certainly not happy about staying home, but then again, maybe Sherlock and his assistant can listen to some classical music and make Mom and Dad feel real guilty so that they can give us a few extra treats. Watson might like that, too. It's important to always look on the bright side. Oh, by the way, don't be surprised by the fact that I enjoy classical music. I am a dog of refined taste in many things. I particularly enjoy Handel and Brahms. Watson hasn't been around here long enough to have developed music preferences.

"Hank," Mom says. "You really don't want to go to the carnival, do you?"

"It's no big deal. Really. I'm just not keen on the rides, but since the twins always have so much fun, I always seem to manage to enjoy myself. I especially like people-watching. Some of the most amazing variety of folks attend a carnival. And you love the rides. Admit it!" He winks. There's another thing that I wish I could do–wink with one eye–not simply blink with two eyes. That I do very well.

A ringing sound is coming from Dad's pocket–his cell phone. "Hank Charles here," he answers. "Hi, Charlie. You guys all ready for the big carnival?"

It sounds like Dad is talking to Mr. O'Brien. He's the Chief of Police. We've all worked together on several occasions. "Yeah, the family and I were planning on heading over in a couple of minutes. Sure...okay...when did you get the call? Where do you want to meet? I hadn't planned on it, but if you don't think it'll be a problem. No, I don't imagine under the circumstances...fifteen minutes...'bye." Dad pushes the 'END' bottom on the phone and stares at the black plastic box in his hand.

"Knock...knock," Mom tries to get Dad's attention.

"I'm sorry," Dad responds. "I was just thinking about what Charlie said."

"Like in Charlie O'Brien?" Mom asks.

"Yes. I apologize. I think I zoned out for a second. He called to ask if we were available to meet him at the carnival."

"We?"

"Yes, the twins and me...and Upton. Something's happened and he'd like us to take a look around. That's okay, isn't it?"

"Of course. Maybe I'll just go on all the rides by myself," Mom kiddingly replies. "All by myself. Sniff."

"Stop being silly. I'm sure it'll only take a couple of minutes; and besides, your input is always welcome. Let me call the twins."

Almost immediately, as if they had overheard Dad, Alex and Veronica bounce into the kitchen.

"Perfect timing," Dad announces. "Get ready to go to the carnival, quickly."

"But if we can only go once, we'd rather go tomorrow. We'll have more time for the rides and besides, all of our friends will be there."

"I think I've heard that before. However, fortunately, you don't have to make the choice, since we've got to go tonight–like right now."

"But Dad," they whine in unison.

The twins are right. Dad had given them the option, and when they try to exercise it, Dad overrules them. That's really not fair.

"We can go tomorrow, also. But we have to go now as well."

14

The twins look at each other and then at Dad–like he has two heads.

"Chief O'Brien called a few minutes ago. There's something he'd like us to look at–all of us. Upton too," Dad explains.

The twins' curiosity is definitely piqued.

What about Watson? She'll probably be better off at home, although she has a lot of potential as a sleuth assistant.

"Consider this a working visit," he continues.

"Hey, less talk and more movement," Mom inserts. "Children, get ready and please bring a light jacket. It may get chilly later this evening. Hank, I'll drive so that I can let you off at the entrance. Parking will be awful on a Friday night."

"Maybe so, but the Chief has a spot waiting for us out front next to his patrol car. Not exactly what I had in mind when I suggested that we have a little celebration."

"What precisely is it that Chief O'Brien wants the Charles clan to investigate?" Mom poses the question.

"He wants us to find something. Actually, to find someone and something. Actually, several somethings." Dad is certainly doing his best to avoid answering the question.

"Okay, wise guy, who or what is missing?"

"The snake lady," Dad reluctantly responds. "And all her snakes."

Right! You've got to be kidding. We're going to a carnival to try and find a whole mess of slithering, slimy snakes. Why bother? Good riddance, if you ask me. Watson will be far better off at home.

"We're ready," Veronica and Alex shout, returning to the kitchen. Each of them is wearing black pants, a black tee shirt, a black ball cap and a black windbreaker. Ninja twins. Oh, they have black fanny packs wrapped around their waists, too.

CHAPTER FIVE
Under the Big Top

The bright lights and pounding sounds of the carnival can be seen and heard blocks away from the park. If we lived near here, I, for one, would certainly find myself searching for some peace and quiet. Like go on a vacation for a couple of days. But, it's only once a year, and everyone really has such a good time. The traffic proceeds at a crawl...a snail's pace, despite the best efforts of the police department to direct cars to the parking areas adjacent to the road. On several occasions, Dad stops to explain to a police officer that Chief O'Brien is expecting us.

Nothing like a late spring evening to bring out the entire town. I'll bet everyone is here. It certainly looks like it. We glide into the reserved parking space and immediately hear, "Thanks for coming." Chief O'Brien rushes over and actually opens the car door for Mom. How cool is that? The Chief of Police helping you out of the car. There is a certain magical feeling about a turning Ferris wheel, a singing merry-go-'round or a bouncing roller coaster.

Yip! I think I had better play it safe. Yip! "What's wrong, Upton?" Dad looks down at me. Then he scans the crowd. "Got it." He bends over and picks me up. Thank goodness he understands what I am 'saying'. I do not relish the thought of being trampled by a herd of people rushing here and there like bees looking for their hive. Furthermore, I can see so much better from up in Dad's arms. And we are supposed to be looking for? I'm not entirely sure what. Hey, I'm only a little white dog, and it's no big deal to carry me around. Right Dad? I give him a little doggie kiss to express my appreciation.

"We're going to meet the show manager at his trailer. He'll give us the basic background," the Chief announces.

"Charlie? Are we supposed to be looking around every corner for a bunch of snakes?" Mom asks.

"No, of course not. Well, I'm not sure. The snake lady and all of her snakes are gone–

presumably together. The travel cases in which the snakes are transported are also gone. So I don't think that they're crawling around the grounds." The Chief is not altogether convincing. "It may be she just decided to take off."

"And leave the carnival?" Alex asks.

"Why would anybody just leave?" Veronica adds.

"Hey kids. Don't jump to conclusions."

"Charlie, you never answered my question, do you know that there are no snakes running– slithering around?" It's no secret that Mom is not fond snakes. Well, truth must be known, neither am I.

"Let's not speculate," Dad says reassuredly. "I'm sure that the carnival manager will be able to fill in the gaps."

Fill in the gaps? The whole thing is gaps. Although Dad always tries to sound logical, sometimes I'm not so sure.

"Follow me!" the Chief commands. "And stay close. It's really crowded." Fortunately that's Dad's problem, not mine. I think I'll readjust myself on his shoulder to get a better view.

"Twins, hold hands," Mom says.

"Mom..." the twins whine in reply. "That's so uncool."

"So is getting lost," Dad suggests.

Reluctantly, Veronica and Alex link arms– with the Chief, who smiles at the way the twins have manipulated the situation. Mom shrugs, but is pleased, because it's unlikely that anything will happen to the twins while walking with the

Chief of Police.

We bob and weave in, out, and around what seems like thousands of people—all moving like giant waves—all in different directions. We pass the tilt-a-whirl, spinning teacups, tunnel of horrors, bumper cars, the cotton candy booth, the fortune teller booth and the hot dog booth. Wait! Can we stop for a minute and maybe get a snack? I sneeze. Just a little hint that food is very much on my mind...for a change.

"Later, Upton," Dad says. "Right now we've got to figure out what happened to the snake lady." And don't forget her snakes.

CHAPTER SIX
Little Tree

After trekking through the grounds, we arrive at a group of trailers that appear to serve as a combination living quarters and administrative center for the carnival.

"Chief!" a voice shouts from a small group of men each of whom is wearing dark coveralls with a stripe on the sleeve. I wish I could tell you the color of the coveralls, but dogs are color blind and like the only reason I know a stop light is red on top, yellow in the middle and green on the bottom is because I heard Mom explaining what the lights mean when the twins were very young. "I'll be right there," the voice continues.

As the meeting breaks up and the men return to doing whatever it is they have been talking about, one remains—the carnival manager. His appearance is...how to remain polite...unique. He isn't even as tall as the twins, and his head is covered with lots and lots of hair, including a large moustache that curls at the ends. Our 'host' is wearing leather pants and a white tee shirt with the words 'Clowns Have More Fun' printed on the front in large letters.

Greeting us with a wave, the manager announces, "Hi! I'm Dimitri Sosolovski. Thank you for coming so promptly, although I didn't expect to see a couple of children and a dog."

"Mr. Sosolovski," the Chief begins, "let me assure you that there are a number of people in jail who have made the mistake of underestimating the Charles family. One cannot judge a book by its cover."

Bowing deeply to the twins, the man says, "I apologize. I should have been more sensitive, especially being a red head."

You mean all that hair and moustache is red. Awesome!

"I'm just a little anxious, I guess. Please call me Tree. And it's not because I'm tall..." The twins smile. "but because I have a name that everyone mispronounces. When I was young, they would call my father, who has the same name, Big Tree, and me...Little Tree. For obvious reasons, I've discontinued using the first part of my nickname." Tree smiles, showing us a mouthful of gold-capped teeth.

"Let me make the introductions," Chief O'Brien offers. "The Charles family: Jackie Charles, and the twins Alex and Veronica." Although the twins are not identical, it's sometimes hard to tell them apart, especially when they are dressed the same—ninja black. "Hank Charles," the Chief continues; "and although last, by no means least, Upton Charles, canine extraordinaire." I sit and extend my paw, which Tree gently shakes.

"Once again, thank you for coming. I'm sorry if I seem upset, but this has never happened before."

"Mr. Sosolovski–Tree, for our benefit please start at the beginning," Dad suggests.

"Amelia is gone and so are all her snakes," sputters the small manager. "She's disappeared. I'm so worried."

Dad rolls his eyes...just a little. "We need to really start at the beginning in order to get a handle on what we can do to help."

"I don't understand. She's not here. She's gone. What else is there to say?"

"Maybe it would be best if we asked you questions," Mom inserts, obviously trying to calm the carnival manager.

"Oh yes...please...ask away. I'll do my best," he quickly replies.

"First of all," Chief O'Brien takes out his notebook, "what is the name of the missing snake charmer?" I hope he doesn't want the names of the snakes as well.

"Amelia."

"Does Amelia have a last name?" Mom asks.

"Oh, of course...Henderson. Amelia Henderson." Tree's eyes dart back and forth between the six of us. He seems very, very nervous.

"Would you be more comfortable talking somewhere else? Somewhere with less distractions?" Mom also senses the fact that Tree is tense.

"Yes. It's a bit too noisy out here. Too much activity. Let's go into my office," he replies, gesturing to the blue and yellow trailer behind us. "It's air conditioned." Funny, I didn't even notice that it was warm outside, and yet Tree's forehead is covered with perspiration.

"That's fine," the Chief answers. "Mobile one to mobile three...over," he calls into his walkie talkie.

"Mobile three. Go ahead, Chief...over."

"Fred, I'm going to be meeting with the carnival manager for the next few minutes and I'll be offline. If you need me, come down to the bright blue trailer at the back of the park...over."

"Got it...over and out," the voice crackles through the black box.

Tree mounts the stairs and unlocks the trailer door. He enters, snaps on the light, and we follow. Unbelievable–simply unbelievable.

CHAPTER SEVEN
Picture Gallery

"Wow!" The twins say in unison.

"Mom, check out the yellow walls. So cool. Can I paint my room?" Veronica is obviously impressed by the décor.

The inside walls of Tree's trailer are painted a very bright color–bright yellow, I guess, and it's furnished with dark leather furniture. Kind of reminds me of a large bumblebee. The interior of the trailer is crammed full of stuff, including photographs of Tree and an older man, his father, 'Big Tree'; posters from circuses and carnivals long gone; and banners with colorful letters announcing 'Amazing Sights and Sounds from the Far Corners of the Globe' which are hung or stacked everywhere.

Trying to catch her breath at the sheer volume of what could be a storage room for the Ringling Brothers Circus Museum, Mom tactfully says, "Wow, this is like, incredible. Tree, where did all this come from?"

"Mostly from shows that Dad, and later I, worked in before he died," Tree slowly replies.

"Look at the picture of you inside a lion's cage," Alex points out.

"And in this one, you're covered with pigeons. Yuck!" Veronica adds.

Tree smiles and starts to walk carefully around the room. "Over here is a picture of Dad and me with former President Clinton. We'd put on a performance on the White House lawn for some disabled children, and we were invited to a reception afterwards. That was special, I must admit."

"What about these people?" Alex asks.

"That's former Soviet Premier, Mikhail Gorbechev, my father, Dimitri Sosolovski the elder, that's his real name, and me, when I was considerably younger. We were touring worldwide with a group of performers from six different countries. It was exciting having the opportunity to visit so many places."

As small as Tree was, his father was tall and thin, clean shaven, and bald. Only their eyes connected them as father and son.

"Who's this?" Mom points to a picture of a beautiful smiling woman with long blonde hair, green eyes that almost sparkle, and a snake wrapped around her shoulders.

"That's..." Tree begins, "that's Amelia." His voice says it all. It is soft and sad.

Taking his cue from the pause in the conversation, Dad suggests, "Maybe we should talk about her. That might give us a place to start our search." Tree nods, still staring at the photograph.

Clearing his throat with a cough, the Chief says, "How long have you known Amelia?"

"A lifetime," Tree absentmindedly responds.

Dad and the Chief exchange glances.

"How long has Amelia been with the carnival?" Dad inquires.

"As long as I have." Two questions–two answers, and absolutely no useful information.

I can sense that the Chief is getting a bit impatient. Mom and Dad both sense it as well. The twins continue to examine the countless pieces of memorabilia from years and years of Tree's life under the big top.

"Who are these people? One of them looks familiar," Veronica shouts. Tree seems to snap out of his trance and swiftly moves toward the small picture hanging next to a large poster of an elephant lifting a lady, with its trunk wrapped around her waist. Mom, Dad, the Chief, and I join them at the photograph. I recognize Tree's father standing next to a petite woman wearing a zebra-striped costume, holding the hands of two small children. A man in a suit has his arm around Big Tree. Everyone is grinning at the camera.

"That's Ike!" Chief O'Brien exclaims. The twins look up at him inquisitively. Me, too.

"Dwight D. Eisenhower, the 34th President of the United States. His nickname was Ike," Dad explains. "During World War II, he was the general in command of all the American soldiers."

"He was a very sweet man," Tree softly adds. "Very kind and gentle. I remember when this picture was taken. It seems like yesterday."

"Is that you?" Alex bounces up and down, pointing at the picture.

"Yes. I can't believe it was over fifty years ago," he continues.

"Who is the woman with the little girl?" Mom asks.

"Oh, that's my mother and Amelia."

"Amelia Henderson?" the Chief stammers.

"Yes. Well, that's her married name. Amelia and I are brother and sister. I'm older... by five minutes."

"You mean you're twins?" Veronica is always excited by the thought of twins. I wonder why? Joke.

"Yes, like you two. In fact, we are opposite in so, so many ways."

CHAPTER EIGHT
Pachyderm Princess

"Tree, we really need to focus on the disappearance of your sister," Dad suggests.

As if he hadn't heard a single word, the red-headed carnival manager begins to talk. "Mother and Father joined the circus in the mid-1930s as teenagers. The Great Depression made finding a job almost impossible for a young man and a young woman. Also, the circus had a certain kind of magnetism–adventure–travel and romance. They met in St. Louis, Missouri in 1938. Dad's show was moving east from California, and the circus with which Mom was working was traveling north for the summer. It must have been love at first sight, because when the two shows each went their separate ways a few days later, my parents were both heading north...together. They toured the country for three years; he worked with cats, while Mom was the Pachyderm Princess."

"What's that?" Alex interrupts.

"Ah," Tree, sighs, pointing to the poster of the lady being lifted by the elephant. "Behold! The Pachyderm Princess, my mother."

"A pachyderm is a fancy name for an elephant," Chief O'Brien inserts for the benefit of the twins.

"Actually Charlie, pachyderm means 'thick-skinned', and applies not only to an elephant, but also to a rhinoceros, or even a pig," Dad tells us. Now that's something I never knew. I always thought that 'pachyderm' and 'elephant' were synonymous. You know, the same. But I'm only a little white dog.

"Tree?" Veronica shyly says.

"Yes, my dear?" he sprightly replies.

"What kind of cats did your father work with?"

"Big cats—primarily lions and tigers. I remember a white leopard once, but mostly lions. Male lions, because they were easier to tame. My father would train them, sometimes raising the lion from a cub. Many of the animals came from another circus, or even a zoo, especially if it was what Dad would call a 'troubled critter'. He was truly gifted. It was like he could talk to the animals," Tree mused.

"Like the dog whisperer?" the twins respond together.

Nodding his head in agreement, Tree replies, "Like the dog whisperer."

The Chief makes a swirling motion with his hand. I think he's suggesting that Tree get on with his story, which is taking a long time, although quite fascinating. I can just imagine Tree and his sister going to school and trying to tell the class how their parents were employed. Cool. They're circus performers.

"Let me try and make a long story somewhat shorter," the miniature manager proposes. "The war came, and because of their love of and skill with animals, both Mom and Dad volunteered to help with the herds of horses maintained by the Army."

"Horses?" Veronica wonders.

"Yes. Actually, the United States Army before the Second World War still had horse-mounted cavalry. At the end of the war, the Germans were so short of fuel for their trucks that they used horses to transport supplies, and even carry troops. Anyway, after the war, Mom and Dad tried to hook up with another circus, but they found that most of the shows were no longer in business. It was even worse in Europe. Where once there had been countless traveling shows, few ever reopened. The hardest thing was to find animals and people who would work long hours for little money."

I hope that Tree covers the next sixty years of his story a lot more quickly than the first twenty, otherwise we'll be here all night and I really need to go out for a walk. Yip!

CHAPTER NINE
The Family Tree

I really feel better. Just a few minutes in the fresh air, together with a couple of doggie things. You know what I mean. I'm ready for the next half-century of the Tree family history. Maybe when he's finally finished, we can then concentrate on the immediately available clues, which are probably getting 'cold'. We need to get at whatever might help us determine what happened to Amelia, the snake lady.

"I know you are all getting restless, so I'll fast forward a bit," our host begins. "When we were twelve, our mother died."

"That must have been terrible for you," Mom inserts.

"It was...for two reasons. First, we all loved her and missed her very, very much; and secondly, because of her death, the circus at which they worked, was forced to close. Not only was Mother gone, but Father had no job."

"Tree...what happened? How did your mother die?" Alex asks.

"There had been a terrible storm—lightning, thunder, and high winds. The animals were terrified. Both Mom and Dad were trying to calm them down when somehow one of Mother's elephants accidentally stepped on her and crushed her to death." Tree stops. He is breathing very quickly. "The police got involved, and they insisted that the poor animal be destroyed because he was a danger—a killer. I remember the elephant. His name was Bert. He was very good around people, he just got scared. Anyway, both Dad and the ring master, who owned the circus, insisted that it was simply an accident. Tragic, but not Bert's fault. In any event, it became a real legal mess, and the show closed. Dad was heartbroken—for Mother—for us, and for his beloved cats. Word got around about the circus folding its tent forever. From out of the blue, someone who remembered my parents from their days working with the Army loaned Father enough money to buy his 'other' children–the lions and tigers. Well, Dad started his own, albeit small, circus, featuring my father and a few remaining members of our big top family. We directed all our energies into the show. We were home-schooled, not only in the traditional subjects like math and history, but also in communicating with the animals around us. Amelia became fascinated with snakes, and I loved birds, especially parrots. The more talkative the better." Tree laughs.

"Although we were a comparatively small show," he continues, "we were very good–authentic and exciting. Dad was always adding new acts, new animals and new people. Everything was great, really great, until Thomas Henderson came into our lives almost twenty years ago. He was tall, dark, and handsome. I hated him the moment I saw him. I knew he was going to be trouble, and he was." The muscles in Tree's jaw tighten up.

Once again, the Chief gestures to make Tree's story move ahead more quickly, but with little effect. The diminutive manager begins to silently pace back and forth across the crowded room. He is clearly angry at the thought of Mr. Henderson. Wait! That's his sister's last name... Henderson.

CHAPTER TEN
Sniffing for Clues

Looking at his watch, Dad, raising one eyebrow in the cool way he does, says at long last, "Tree, we really must get to the present. Not only is it getting late, but whatever physical evidence that may help us locate your sister is being contaminated as we speak."

"Yes...yes. I just thought you should know the background behind Amelia's disappearance." I agree that background information is often useful; however, putting one's nose to the ground, both literally and figuratively, is far more useful.

"I'll make it quick. I promise. Thomas Henderson wormed his way into my sister's affections, and after about two years of doing nothing to help, he talked her into running away with him. I mean, like without so much as telling Father or me. Like a thief sneaking off in the dark. It almost broke Dad's spirit, not to mention his heart, once again. We muddled on, but the spark was gone. Both Father and the animals were getting older, and one day about five years ago, Big Tree simply gave up. I think the words 'the show must go on' had lost their meaning to him. Anyway, I decided that I couldn't handle the circus by myself, so I downscaled to what you see now: an automated carnival with a few sideshows, like Amelia's snakes, but no large animal acts, no clowns, and no big top. I've been very successful, which leads me back to Amelia and Thomas Henderson."

Thank goodness. Everyone lets out a collective sigh of relief.

"A couple of years ago, without any kind of notice, Henderson and my sister waltz back into my life. Amelia looked horrid. She was tired and thin—very thin. He was looking for a job, preferably one that paid well and required him to do nothing. It took all the self-control I had not to strangle him, but out of love for my sister, I relented and actually gave him a position. Within a month I regretted my decision. I started to notice that the money from tickets and rides had decreased substantially, while at the same time we were doing booming business. I suspected someone was stealing from us, and that the someone was Henderson. I confronted him, and he laughed at me. He admitted that he took money from the register whenever he 'needed a few bucks'. I fired him right then and there. When he told my sister that he had been dismissed, she told him that she was staying with me and the carnival. Well, he stormed out and she remained...until today. I don't know why she's gone. We've been really happy the past few years. She had a lot of friends and was always talking to someone, reading something, going somewhere. We close the show during January, and she and I have traveled to Europe and to the Caribbean. I had even heard that Henderson had gotten in some trouble up North. To the best of my knowledge, he never tried to contact Amelia after he left. That is, until a couple of days ago."

"A couple of days ago?" Mom and Dad say together.

"Yes, she received some kind of package. I didn't think much about it at the time, but it seemed to upset her–really upset her, but the worst seemed to pass in a few minutes."

"Did you notice anything different about her behavior after that?" Dad quickly asks.

Now we're getting to the really important stuff–like who, what, where, when, how, and why. Answer these six questions and the riddle is solved. Maybe we should try and find the package Amelia received and check it out.

CHAPTER ELEVEN
Coincidence?

"Let me think. By late afternoon yesterday, we had pretty much set up the carnival for today's opening. Amelia's act is self-contained, so she was ready to go by noon. I guess that's when I saw her last. It was noon yesterday."

"What do you mean, self-contained?" Alex exclaims. I'm glad she asks the question, because I don't know what he means either.

"Amelia has her own trailer. She has a sleeping section, a section for her snakes, and a section that pulls out, where she can perform with her reptiles. She takes care of everything herself. I really don't pay any attention to her during setup, which is a relief, since I have so much to do with everything else. Anyway, I don't remember seeing her since then. I thought it a little strange, because normally we would have dinner together; but as I said before, ever since she got that package she hasn't been herself. You know, a bit off."

"Off?" Dad asks.

"She was not her upbeat self. Seemed more distant. Actually, I didn't think much about it because I had so many other things on my mind," Tree continues.

"Like what?" Chief O'Brien asks. Actually he kind of demands. I'm not sure if what Tree has on his mind is relevant, but he is the Chief of Police and I am only a little white dog. But still...

"Huh? Oh, between opening the show, making sure everything is ready to go, paying the bills, confirming the schedule for the next couple of months, worrying about the weather, which is one thing I can't control. There's a lot to think about. Especially the weather. It's the one thing that affects us the most. Bad weather means no people, which means no money. There's just a ton of things," Tree hesitantly replies. I sense he's not telling us everything. Just call it canine intuition, but there's something else.

"Anything else?" Mom gazes directly at Tree in the same way she looks at the twins when she knows they're not telling her the entire truth.

"Why...yes," he slowly considers. "It's mostly all the little details that require my attention each day."

"Are you sure?" Dad joins in, sounding a bit skeptical as well.

If we were outside, I think the red-headed carnival man would try to find a bush and disappear behind it. That's funny, a Tree in a bush. Okay, it's a bad joke. A really bad joke. There's simply no place to hide inside a crowded trailer.

"I guess there's one more thing," Tree meekly adds.

"Yes?" Mom and Dad respond together.

"I'm not sure where to begin."

"Just try and get to the end...quickly," the Chief harshly inserts. I guess he's getting impatient, which I understand. We've spent over an hour and aren't even started.

"It's...it's really nothing to do with Amelia...much," Tree sputters.

"Please," Dad begins. "Let us be the judge of that. We need all the facts, whether they seem relevant or not. Sometimes, a little detail will show us where to place a piece of the puzzle. Please, Tree, we are trying to help locate your sister, but you've got to help us."

"I received an offer to sell the carnival," Tree whispers.

"When?" The Chief turns toward the now very nervous brother of the missing snake lady.

"A couple of days ago. In fact, the same day that Amelia got her package. I remember because I was selfishly more concerned with my mail than hers," he admits.

I'm trying to make the connection between the package, Amelia's disappearance, and the offer to purchase the carnival. Coincidence? Probably, but I don't really believe in coincidence. So there must be a connection, but I can't figure it out. However, it's still early in our investigation, although getting late in the evening.

"You make it sound like it's a bad thing that someone is trying to buy the carnival. Is there something else in the offer?" Dad persists.

"Yes and no."

"Stop!" the Chief bellows. "I am not going to waste the resources of our police department, including imposing upon the Charles family, if you are going to be evasive. I'll simply note that your sister decided to leave on her own accord. Obviously, in the event something turns up, we'll deal with it then. I'm out of here." I can imagine the steam coming from the Chief's ears. He puts a whole new dimension to the expression 'hot under the collar'.

"It's not what you think," the diminutive manager explains. "It's not."

"Then what is it?" Mom interrupts, once again staring in the way only a mother can stare— like right through you.

"The offer is for a lot of money," he begins.

So what? Isn't that the purpose of selling something to sell it for a lot of money? The carnival looks like a successful business, so what's the big deal that someone wants to buy it?

"I'm not following," the Chief blurts out, taking two quick steps toward Tree, who seems to shrink to even smaller proportions than before. "It seems to me that if the offer wasn't for a lot of money, you wouldn't even be thinking about it. So, and it's last time I'm going to ask, what's going on?"

"We are doing well here, and the carnival is probably worth a lot of money to the right people. I work sixteen to eighteen hours a day on average, seven days a week. Even during the month we take off in the winter, we're always checking out other shows looking for new talent and new ideas. Quite frankly, I'm getting tired, and not any younger."

"Tree, please don't be so defensive. No one is criticizing you for considering a sale. No one is implying that you haven't worked extremely hard all your life and that maybe it's time to slow down. Please relax and just tell us the facts—plain and simple. Once again, we're in a far better position to decide what's important and what's not than you are." Dad is trying to sound reassuring, but somehow it's having the opposite effect on Tree.

"The problem with the offer is that it is too high. It's too good to be true, so I checked out the potential buyer. It's a corporation, a foreign corporation with plenty of money behind it."

"That certainly doesn't seem like a problem to me," Dad suggests.

"Maybe not, but my instinct tells me there's something funny going on. Why would this company be interested in my carnival? Why?"

Dad raises one eyebrow. The rest of us just look at one another, and then at Tree in disbelief. This investigation is going nowhere...fast...or rather, slowly.

CHAPTER TWELVE
Suspicious Character

"Is there anything special about the offer other than the price?" Dad begins to walk back and forth, as much as you can in a crowded trailer. "Is there anything–anything at all that you can think of that explains your negative reaction to the proposal to buy the carnival?"

Tree starts to move his foot back and forth, like he's thinking. "I saw him! Well, I think I saw him. At the show last weekend. He was just hanging around. Moving around the carnival.

I watched him for about an hour. He didn't do anything except walk around and then he left."

"Who?" Mom, Dad, the Chief and the twins all ask at the same time.

"Him! At least I think it was him. He'd grown a beard since the last time I'd seen him, but I'm pretty sure it was him." Tree's voice is loud and he sounds very angry. His hands start to shake.

"Him?" Dad asks. "Do you mean Henderson, your sister's husband?"

"Ex-husband. She got divorced from him," Tree immediately replies.

This is getting interesting, although I can't say we're any further along in the investigation except there's a potential answer to 'who'.

"Assuming that Henderson showed up last week, he didn't try to make any contact with your sister or you, did he?" The Chief is speaking, well yelling even louder than Tree.

"Not that I know of. He never talked to me and Amelia never mentioned she either saw or heard from him."

"Tree," Mom softly begins. "Why do you think that the offer to purchase the carnival and the possible, even definite sighting of Henderson have anything to do with one another?"

Excellent question Mom. Even if Henderson showed up to check out the show, what could that have to do with the sale?

Tree walks over to a small refrigerator sitting in the corner of the trailer, covered by piles of papers. "Anyone care for a drink? Water...

soda...juice...iced tea?" His voice is calmer.

"Mom?" The twins ask.

"Sure," she responds.

"Do you have orange soda?" Alex walks over toward the open refrigerator.

"Here you go." Tree hands him a bottle. "It's from Italy. Fabulous tasting. You're Alex, right?" He nods. He turns. "And you Veronica?"

"Grape?" She says hesitantly.

"Sure. Same thing...Italian." Tree hands Veronica a bottle.

"I can't get it open," Alex announces.

"Sorry. It needs a bottle opener. It's not twist off." He reaches into his pocket and pulls out a small shining object, which he holds up and says, "it's a church key."

I thought the twins needed a bottle opener, not a key, especially one to open a church.

"Church key?" Veronica sounds confused. So am I.

"When we were kids," Dad says, "we used to call bottle openers 'church keys'. I don't remember why. Charlie?"

"I never thought about it. If you needed to open a bottle or a can, you asked for a church key."

"I don't mean to interrupt this trip down memory lane, but I think we should get back to the question—why do you think that Mr. Henderson is somehow connected with the offer to purchase the carnival?" I'm glad Mom is bringing us back to the investigation, especially since no one asked me if I wanted something to Tree reaches into

the refrigerator and retrieves a bottle of water.
"Anyone else?"

CHAPTER THIRTEEN
Slimy like a Snake

"Tree?" Dad is beginning to sound impatient.

"I told you this guy is slimy. He's so slimy he makes one of Amelia's snakes look good. Henderson always had a scheme. Who could he cheat next. He thought he could use Amelia to get the show to be his personal bank, except it was a one way relationship–withdrawals, but never deposits. He kept reading these books about off shore companies. Corporations in Bahamas with trusts in the Caymans and accounts in Panama. You know the kind of stuff I'm talking about." Tree is very animated again.

Frankly, I don't understand a single word he's just said.

"Dad?" Alex moves away from her sister. "I don't understand what Tree is talking about."

"Me neither," Veronica adds.

That makes three of us.

"Simply said and I think I'm right, Tree believes that his former brother in law might be involved in the group that is trying to buy the carnival. Although I think his explanation is a bit far reaching, the timing of the offer, Mr. Henderson showing up last week, the package Amelia received and her disappearance may be connected or may be a coincidence and nothing has to do with the other. That's what we have to find out."

Now that's as clear as mud. Remember, I don't believe in coincidence, especially when we are investigating. Okay, let's start investigating. Where's Amelia's trailer. I need to sniff around. I really hope that Tree is right that all the snakes are gone. Hello? Yip!

"What is it Upton?" Mom asks.

"I think he wants to get down to business."

Chief O'Brien, you are absolutely correct.

"Tree, we need to examine physical evidence. Eliminate what is not relevant and concentrate on what fits together. What is there? The offer to buy, the package Amelia received, her trailer, and whatever else you can think of.

You've got to help us Tree. Concentrate."

Yea! I think we're going in the right direction–clues.

"Mobile One to Mobile Three...over." The Chief suddenly says into the black box on his shoulder.

"Mobile Three. Yes Chief...over." The box crackles.

"Where's Jenkins...over?"

Great! He's trying to find Detective Jenkins. We've worked with him before and he's real smart and real nice.

"Right here, sir...over." The voice of Ted Jenkins comes through loud and clear.

"It's Mr. Jenkins," the twins say together. I think they like him a lot.

"Mobile One to Mobile Three. Jenkins, got your computer?"

"I never leave home without it, Chief... over."

"Meet us at the snake trailer in..." Chief O'Brien looks at Dad whole holds up an open hand. "five minutes...over."

"Understood. Mobile Three...over and out." "Tree, do you have anything with Mr. Henderson's handwriting?" Dad asks.

"Do have a picture?" Veronica is getting into the case.

"Or a picture of your sister? Like a new one." Alex adds.

"And anything you've received from the people who want to buy the carnival." Mom joins in.

How about the envelope from the people? Or the package Amelia got. Mr. Jenkins is great at finding fingerprints. I guess it's time to head over to the snake trailer. Maybe I can do a few doggy things on the way over. Good thing I didn't ask for anything to drink. Yip!

"You're right, Upton. Time to go and do some real sleuthing." Dad looks toward Tree, who is pushing papers off the top of what may be a desk, if you can find it.

"Got it! Let's go!" He hold up a thick big envelope.

Come to think about it, I wonder if you can get fingerprints from paper? Detective Jenkins will know.

CHAPTER FOURTEEN
Down to Business

Fortunately Amelia's trailer is completely on the other side of the carnival, which gives me time and places to do what I've got to do. What a relief.

"I've got an extra set of keys," Tree announces.

It never occurred to me that he wouldn't have a key until I realized that I wouldn't want a key to a place where snakes are crawling all around. The trailer looks like...a snake trailer.

The entire length is painted with snakes–large, small, in trees, on the ground, all coiled up and each and every snake looks scary. I can't understand how something so frightening can be so interesting to so many people.

"Amelia's snakes are...were the most popular exhibit of the carnival," Tree proudly says.

"More popular than the 'Hammer'?" Alex asks.

"Actually...yes. Only kids like your age would ride the 'Hammer' more than once, but lots of people came to see the snakes. Amelia's show changed all the time so that no two were exactly the same and that's what made it great. People could only expect one thing from my sister–the unexpected." Tree pauses and sadly looks at the key in his hand. "I miss her already and it's only been a couple of hours."

"Sorry to break up the party." Detective Jenkins walks toward us with his lap top over one shoulder and his evidence bag over the other. He's carrying so much stuff. He looks like he's going on a vacation.

"Enter the snake pit," Tree says unlocking the trailer door. I don't think he's got a very good sense of humor.

The Chief, Detective Jenkins and Dad follow the small carnival owner into the dark trailer. Mom, the twins and I slowly approach the door. Suddenly the lights go on inside the trailer.

"It's okay," Dad shouts. "The Chief has got the rattlesnake cornered."

Rattlesnakes are very dangerous because if they bite you, their sharp fangs release a poison that can be fatal. I remember a program on TV that said rattlesnakes eat small animals and I'm a small animal. I also remember hearing that before they bite, they rattle their tails. I don't hear anything.

"Hank Charles!" Mom shouts. "This is not amusing. I hate snakes, but I'm trying to help you find Amelia Henderson. No jokes. Is there a snake in the trailer or not?" Mom is really upset. I don't blame her.

"Sorry." I think Dad realizes that he is not being funny. "The place is empty. Like totally empty. It's fine to come in."

Cautiously, we each enter the trailer. It is empty. Except for a bed, a bureau, what looks like a work table, a couple of folding chairs, there's nothing to look at.

"Where is everything?" Tree screams

"Please take a deep breath," Chief O'Brien advises. "Try and tell us what was here before your sister disappeared. What she took or should I say, what is missing. It might be very important." The Chief is talking softly and slowly. Usually he talks loudly and quickly.

While everyone is crowded around Tree, waiting for him to tell us what should be here, Detective Jenkins has already opened his bags, placed the lap top on the table and is booting it up.

"Chief, I'm going to dust the place for fingerprints," he says while opening his evidence bag.

I think I should do some exploring also. Yip! I start to walk toward the back of the trailer and then walk back to where everyone is standing.

"Good idea, Upton. Check it out." I think that Chief O'Brien is beginning to understand me.

"Did you just talk to the dog?" Tree asks.

"He asked me a question, so I thought it polite to answer." Despite the seriousness of the situation, I think the Chief is playing a little joke on the little man.

"He asked you a question?" Clearly the carnival owner is confused.

"Yes. Didn't you hear him?" The Chief is clearly enjoying this conversation.

"He yipped. That's all he did."

"He yipped *do you want me to check out the trailer?*" It's probably time to stop this and get down to business.

"Tree, it's why the Chief asked us here in the first place. We have worked together before and..."

"Successfully," the Chief interrupts.

"Upton is part of the team and seems to know exactly what he should do. He was simply telling us that he was going to explore the trailer."

Seems to know, of course, I know. Oh well, Dad was paying me a compliment. I think. In any event, it's getting late and the carnival is going to be closing in a little while. I hope the twins weren't planning to go on any rides tonight. They haven't said anything. I understand why. They've moved over to help Detective Jenkins. Time to get down to some serious sniffing.

CHAPTER FIFTEEN
Gone Without a Smell

"Like everything is gone!" Tree franticly walks around the trailer. His head swivels from side to side.

"Prior to today, when is the last time you were in your sister's trailer?" The Chief is trying to calm down the carnival owner.

"Let's see. We had dinner together on Wednesday. That was two days ago, but I didn't actually go in. Everyone who works for the carnival eats together in the dining trailer.

Amelia and I ate alone that night so that we could talk about the offer. She seemed distant, but she's like that sometimes. We walked back here, said good night and that's it."

"Tree," Dad inserts. "Please try and answer the question. When were you last in Amelia's trailer, not when was the last time you weren't in her trailer."

I want to hear what Tree has to say, but I also want to check out what I can.

"Before we got here. I was in the trailer then. Last Saturday. One of her snakes had died. Amelia was very upset and I tried to console her. She thought it had been poisoned or something."

Now that's a thought, a poisonous snake being poisoned. Is that even possible?

"Okay, what was in the trailer?" The Chief wants an answer.

"All the snake cages–maybe twenty; and two big trunks filled with costumes and other things for her show. Also the bureau had her regular things–like clothes. She had an old stuffed teddy bear on her bed. Mom had given one to each of us. I still have mine, too." Tree looks down at the floor. "Wait!" He shouts. Her jewelry box is missing. And her file box. She used to keep articles and letters and important papers in the box."

"That's it?" Mom seems a little surprised. Compared to Mom's closets, Amelia's trailer must seem so small.

"Oh," Tree says. "Most of Amelia's stuff is stored at a friend's house. We're on the road for thirty weeks each season. We don't really need much. Just whatever is necessary for the show. When we decided to go to Europe, Amelia packed two of the largest suitcases you ever saw and we were only going for ten days."

Mom probably feels better. Traveling light is not something Mom does.

Time is wasting. I start at the door and slowly and carefully walk around the edge of Amelia's home away from home. I don't want to think that the trailer was also home for a bunch of snakes. I wonder what a snake smells like? I confess I have no experience in herpetology–that's the name for the study of snakes. Pretty big word for a little dog. Back to business.

"Chief, we've got several different prints," Detective Jenkins announces. "Both complete and partials. The twins and I will run them to see what we can find."

"What in the world did he just say?" I don't think carnival people are familiar with the world of modern fingerprint technology.

"Sorry," Detective Jenkins replies. "I have been able to find and remove fingerprints from what looks like three different people. I have also found some fingerprints that are not complete–a tip of finger or a side–like someone holding something very carefully between their fingers. I can compare the partials with the complete fingerprints to see if they belong to the same person or possibly yet another person. I can scan the complete fingerprints into the computer and check the local, state and federal data bases for a match."

"How would fingerprints get into the database?" Tree asks an excellent question.

I think Detective Jenkins likes to talk about crime solving. He'd make a good teacher. "Fingerprints get into data bases in several different ways. Sometimes if you need a license or permit for a firearm, or in some places for a driver's license or fishing or hunting license, your fingerprints are taken. Also if you are in the military or get into trouble, your fingerprints are taken. We have a program in town that encourages parents to bring in children to the police department to have their children's fingerprints taken, so they can be identified if they get lost or something."

I wonder if they should do the same thing for dogs. What if I get lost or something? Maybe that's why I wear the metal tag with my name and our phone number on my collar. If I stop to listen to what's going on, I'll never finish my job.

What's that?

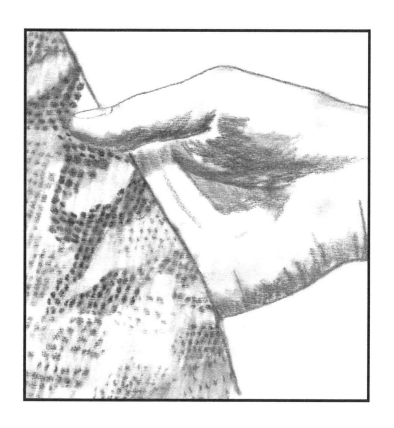

CHAPTER SIXTEEN
The Nose...Knows

That's a smell I'm not likely to ever forget. It's not gross–like real stinky. It's just...different. Yip!

"What is it Upton?" Dad quickly crosses the trailer to where I am standing.

Yip! I begin to scratch the wall near the smell.

"Looks like he's on the trail of something," Chief O'Brien adds.

"Tree, is there anything behind these

walls?" Dad starts to knock along the bottom of the trailer.

"I don't think so," replies Tree who is pacing back and forth.

"Let's remove a panel," suggests Detective Jenkins who joins us. "I've got a screwdriver in my evidence case."

There are simply too many people in one very small part of a very small trailer and I don't feel like being stepped on. I'll keep sniffing while everyone else watches Detective Jenkins remove the wall panel. Nothing...nothing...nothing... wait! Same smell. Yip!

"Give us a minute Upton. I want to see what's behind this wall first." Dad makes sense. Do one thing at a time.

I decide that I'll defer additional snooping until I can see the source of the first smell.

"Chief, can you give me a hand?" Detective Jenkins is trying to pull the wall panel. Sometimes Chief O'Brien does some really dumb things. He starts to clap. You know when someone says 'let's give the winner a hand' it means to clap. I don't think Detective Jenkins was using the word that way.

"Charlie, it's getting late. It's past the twins' bedtime." Mom doesn't think the clapping was the least bit funny either.

"Mom, it's Friday and we can sleep late tomorrow," the twins respond in unison.

"Okay...okay. Let me help you Jenkins." Together the two men remove a section of the trailer wall.

"A snake!" Mom screams.

"No dear, a former snake." Dad picks up the object now resting on the floor. "To be more precise, a snake skin." Dad holds it up for everyone to see. The skin is light colored with dark bands across the surface.

It looks like a snake, but without the snake. It's the outside of the snake. Where's the rest of it?

"It's perfectly normal." Tree walks over to Dad. The snake skin is longer than Tree is tall. "It's from a boa constrictor. One of Amelia's favorite. When the snake grows too large for it's skin, it sheds the old one and grows a bigger skin."

No way! That skin has got to be five feet long and it needs a bigger one?

"Mr. Tree, I have a question." Veronica raises her hand like she does in school.

"Yes, Veronica." Tree guesses correctly.

"How big do boa constrictors get?"

"Sometimes as long as ten to twelve feet long," he answers.

"How big was...is this boa constrictor?" Alex sounds like I feel. A little nervous that a giant snake is hiding somewhere.

"Bullet is only about six feet long. He's still a baby," Tree says.

"Bullet?" Dad raises one eye brow.

"Amelia names all her snakes," the carnival owner responds.

I wish I could communicate more effectively. I really want to know how–Bullet got behind the wall and where is he now. Hey! What about the other smelly place. Yip!

"Good point Upton. Let's check out the other wall section. Where is it big guy." I love it when Dad calls me big guy instead of when the twins call me baby dog. Follow me.

"Mr. Tree, can I ask another question?" Veronica says. "How'd the snake get behind the wall if it's almost six feet long?"

"A snake can squeeze through a very small hole. Bullet probably was looking for a private spot to shed his skin."

I wonder what the snake was doing outside of its cage in the first place.

CHAPTER SEVENTEEN
It's Getting Late

Detective Jenkins removes the second wall panel, only to find another snake skin. A lot smaller than the python. I just can't bring myself to say call the snake by his name–Bullet. I've still got some wall sniffing to do, but it is not very encouraging. The place is really empty and that means no clues.

"Hank, it's getting late." Mom looks at her watch. "...and the twins need to get to bed."

"Not yet. We're not   tired." The twins'

response is predictable. It's been like that for as long as I can remember. They could be falling over–half asleep and they'd say the same thing.

"Unfortunately," the Chief begins, "we're not closer to finding Amelia and her snakes than we were several hours ago."

"I disagree, Chief." Detective Jenkins walks over to the table on which he had put his laptop. He clicks on the screen. "We've got at least two ID's. Thomas Henderson and Dimitri Soslovski."

"That's me!" Tree announces.

"And Henderson is your sister's ex-husband, correct?" Dad isn't really asking.

"Jenkins, where'd the match come from?" I don't really understand the Chief's question.

"Charlie," Mom says, "what do you mean 'come from'?" I am so happy Mom asked.

"If I might answer," Detective Jenkins says. "One set of fingerprints came from the Bureau of Prisons and the other from the Sarasota County Sheriff's office in Florida."

I guess that answers the question about Mr. Henderson getting in trouble, but it sounds like Tree was in trouble also.

"Would care to explain why your finger prints are on record?" The Chief turns toward Tree and stands up real straight to look bigger.

"No problem." Tree pulls his wallet out of his pocket. "Sarasota is the winter headquarters of the Ringling Brothers Circus. Most of us in the circus business call Sarasota home. We try to do a number of shows there before heading on tour.

"That doesn't quite answer the question," Dad says.

"Oh, the fingerprints. There is a law or something that says that anyone who handles animals that are displayed to the public needs a permit and you get it from the Sheriff and see..." Tree hands the Chief a piece of paper. "it's got my name, address, picture and fingerprint. Well, actually only my thumb print, but they put ink on all my fingers and made me push each finger on a card."

Alex raises her hand.

"Yes, young man," the Chief says.

"If you got a permit to handle animals, wouldn't your sister have one also?"

Excellent! I'm proud of Alex.

"You know, you're absolutely right. I remember one time when we had to get a new permit, we went down together."

"That's very helpful," Detective Jenkins adds. "I can get them to download the fingerprint card and maybe one of the partials will match."

"I'm troubled." Mom starts to walk around the trailer. "How can someone live in a trailer, a small trailer and not leave fingerprints all over the place?"

Another great question.

"There are a lot of fingerprint smudges all over the trailer. But they are only smudges." Detective Jenkins pushes some keys on his computer. "I only lifted the prints that were clear. The others cannot be used for identification, but there are definitely prints from at least one other person."

This time Veronica raises her hand.

"Yes, Veronica," Dad says.

"Are the prints you found on top of the other prints?"

I think I see where she's going with her question.

"Why yes they are." The detective is trying to follow.

"Will you tell us what you're thinking." Chief O'Brien is also confused.

"Well, if the fingerprints of Mr. Henderson and Tree were on top of other fingerprints, maybe Amelia's, doesn't that mean they were here after she had already left?"

"Amazing," Tree says. "She's right. I came by the trailer to look for Amelia early this afternoon when I couldn't find her."

"Tree, you acted so surprised when we entered the trailer and found everything was gone." Dad's right.

"I never went inside. I knocked a couple of times. I really don't like going into her trailer. It's rude unless you're invited in and besides, I really don't like snakes. I did think about opening the door and even grabbed the door knob, but I never went in. Besides, someone called me to look at something and I left."

"Jenkins...your thoughts." Chief O'Brien isn't sure that Mr. Tree is telling the truth.

"Only print I found from Mr. Sosolovski was on the door knob."

"Please call me Tree. It's so much easier."

Detective Jenkins nods. "Mr. Henderson's prints were on the light switch inside, on the edge of the door and the door knob. His prints covered all but one print from Tree."

"That means..." Dad starts.

"He was the last one here." The twins shout together.

"And the place was empty when he got here." Mom walks quickly around the trailer.

"Do you think Amelia knew that Henderson was around and left before he got here?" Tree is obviously concerned about his sister.

If Amelia was scared and left, that doesn't explain the package she got and Mr. Henderson hanging around the carnival last week. Or does it? The problem is that we don't have any idea where she went, whether Mr. Henderson knows where she is or whether he followed her. And why? There's got to be some kind of clue that I haven't found...yet.

CHAPTER EIGHTEEN
First Real Clue

"I think it's time to go," Mom says. "I'm not sure what else we can accomplish tonight and it's getting late."

I'm not sure what we can accomplish–period. There doesn't appear to be anything to help our investigation except that Mr. Henderson was in Amelia's trailer after she'd already left. Maybe we should look for Mr. Henderson, but how?

"Children..." Dad always calls the twins

'children' when he's about to say something important. "Mom's right, it's time to go."

"Please," Veronica and Alex plead. "A few more minutes. We've been good and tomorrow's Saturday."

There is no question that they've been good and as I recall they used the Saturday argument a little while ago.

"Maybe things will be clearer in the morning." Tree doesn't sound convinced, although he's trying to be optimistic.

Mom opens the door in an effort to get everyone moving. Since I have a few doggie things to take of, I dash past her. The fresh air feels good. I didn't like being cooped up in the trailer. The thought that snakes live–lived there is creepy. While I've got a few minutes I'll check around the outside of the trailer.

"Come on twins." Good luck Mom.

Nothing...nothing at all. The outside of the trailer smells exactly the same all around. Slowly I head back to the front door, which Mom is still holding open. Wait a minute! Yip!

"What is it Upton," Dad asks from inside the trailer.

Yip!

"Let's see what he's found." Chief O'Brien leads everyone out of the snake place.

Yip! I paw the ground carefully so that I don't disturb my new discovery.

"Let's take a look." Dad bends down. "Detective Jenkins," he calls, "take a look at this." The detective removes a pair of tweezers from his pocket and picks up the object.

"A matchbook," he announces. He turns it over. "... from the Macaw Inn."

"That's the new place on the beach," the Chief says.

Looking at Tree Dad asks, "does your sister smoke?"

"No and neither do I, but Thomas Henderson is a heavy smoker. His clothing always smelled like stale cigarette smoke."

That must be an unattractive smell. I'm glad Mom and Dad don't smoke. Ugh!

"I'm going to see if I can lift a print from the matchbook. It'll only take a minute."

"Mom, may we please get some cotton candy?" Alex asks.

"Like before they close the carnival," Veronica adds.

"Why not? I'm very curious what Detective Jenkins finds and we've got a few minutes. Let's go!" Mom sounds excited.

"My treat! Follow me!" Tree's spirits seem to have lifted.

The thought of eating cotton candy does not appeal to me. Maybe because it's so sticky. I actually tried it once and I got pink goo all over my hair. A Bichon Frise has hair not fur like most dogs. Every two weeks I get a shampoo and blow dry and sometimes a haircut. Anyway, I still haven't taken care of those doggie things I wanted to do.

"Honey, I'll stay here with the Chief and Detective Jenkins and Upton. See you in a bit."

Dad waves as the three members of the Charles clan and the diminutive carnival owner march off toward the food tent.

CHAPTER NINETEEN
A Match

I use the time wisely and feel a lot better. I hope Detective Jenkins can find, remove and identify a fingerprint from the matchbook I found. I wonder what's the significance that it says 'Macaw Inn' on the cover?

"Hey Dad, want a bit of my cotton candy?" Alex is running toward the trailer holding a half eaten cotton candy cone.

"No thanks, Alex," Dad politely replies.

"You can have some of mine if you'd

like," Veronica offers. "I think Alex' blue cotton candy is disgusting."

Now that's something I never knew. Cotton candy comes in different colors.

"Veronica, the color doesn't change the taste. It's only food coloring." Mom hands a cup to Dad. "Root beer. I thought you might be thirsty. Tree is bringing drinks for the Chief and Detective Jenkins and a bottle of water for you, Upton."

That's very thoughtful. All this investigative work makes me a little thirsty.

"Very interesting. Very interesting." Detective Jenkins says from inside the trailer.

Putting down his cell phone, Chief O'Brien says, "what did you find Jenkins?"

"A match. Thomas Henderson." Detective Jenkins is pleased.

"Now what?" Mom asks.

"Charlie, I think you should call the Macaw Inn and see if Mr. Henderson is registered," Dad suggests.

"Good idea, Hank." The Chief looks down at the match book and says, "how convenient, the number is right here." He starts to push the number into his cell phone.

"Wait!" Tree, who has entered the trailer unnoticed, screams. "Wait!"

"Why?" Mom asks.

"Yes, why?" The tone of the Chief's voice lowers.

"If he is registered, we need to find out if he's there," Tree states.

"Of course I'm going to try and find out if he's there." The Chief sounds annoyed.

"We need to talk to him!" Tree is almost frantic.

"That's why I'm calling," answers Chief O'Brien.

"But if he's there, what if he leaves before we get there?" Tree is beginning to make sense. "I know he knows where Amelia is."

"Tree, please take a deep breath. The Chief knows what he's doing. Although it might take us twenty minutes to get over to the Inn, the Chief can get a squad car there in...twenty seconds. Well, within a minute or two." Dad sounds reassuring.

"May I call now?" The Chief is trying to be calm as well.

Tree nods his head as the Chief redials the Inn's number.

"Good evening, this is Chief O'Brien. Do you have a Mr. Thomas Henderson registered as a guest at the Inn?" Everyone moves a little closer to the Chief. "How long ago?" There is a long pause while the person from the Inn is talking.

"Thank you. Please do not mention this call to anyone. I don't want to alarm any of the people staying at the Inn, including Mr. Henderson."

The Chief closes his cell phone. "He's there. Well, he was there. He's registered but he went out with a woman about an hour ago. Your sister," he turns toward Tree, "...based on the description the man at the desk just gave me."

"Is she...is she okay?" Tree stammers.

"It appears as though your sister arrived alone and met Henderson and they left together... in his car." Chief O'Brien looks at each of us. "A black Lincoln Town Car with New York plates... vanity type plates. SNKCHRMR."

What does that mean? SNKCHRMR? I wish I was better at words, but I'm only three, and a dog.

"Hank?" Chief O'Brien seems a puzzled as I am.

Before Dad can say a thing, the twins shout, together as they often do, "I've got it!"

"Kids...slowly...one at a time."

"Me first!" Alex says. "I'm oldest."

"Not fair!" Veronica replies. "You're only older by one minute. Anyway I got it first."

"Hold it!" Mom doesn't like the twins arguing. "Hank, do you have a piece of paper and a pen?"

Detective Jenkins, who is smiling at the exchange between Veronica and Alex says, "Here is a piece of paper and a pencil for each of you. Write down what you think the license plate means."

Each quickly writes down the answer and hands it to Mom. She opens each paper and begins to laugh. "Very good." Mom gives the papers to Dad who gives them to the Chief. What about me? Yip!

"I think Upton wants to know the answer... as do I." Tree is beginning to understand me.

"SNKCHRMR–snake charmer. Son of a

gun" Chief O'Brien holds up the twins' answer.

"Snake charmer...snake charmer...more like snake oil." Tree screams.

What is snake oil? Sounds gross.

"Mobile one to base...over." Chief O'Brien says into his walkie talkie.

"Base to mobile one. What's up Chief? Over." The little black box answers.

"I want an APB on a Black Lincoln Town Car, New York plate SNKCHRMR. Observe, tail, but don't apprehend. Over."

"What kind of nut has the license plate snake charmer? Over"

"Don't worry about it, just get it out now... over and out."

"Chief...sir, please tell me what you just said." Tree isn't used to the way the police talk.

"May I?" Detective Jenkins offers. The chief nods. "APB is an all points bulletin to state and local police to look for Mr. Henderson's car. They are to report when they find it, follow it without being seen, but do not stop it."

Cool. I think this is getting exciting. But what about the snakes?

CHAPTER TWENTY
SNKCHRMR

"I don't mean to sound like a party pooper, but the twins have got to get to bed." Mom points at her watch.

"Not now," Veronica says.

"It's almost over," Alex adds.

"We have no idea how long it will take the police to find Mr. Henderson's car. It might be hours or not at all."

Mom does have a valid point. Just because the Chief is trying to find the snake charmer, it doesn't mean he will–at least not soon. Wait a minute! If Amelia Henderson is a real snake charmer, why does Mr. Henderson's plate say SNKCHRMR. I wonder if he worked with snakes as well as Amelia. That might explain the missing snakes. How am I going to get someone to ask the question. Maybe a little bark or a sneeze. It's a real problem when you don't have the ability to communicate in words. Maybe if I just think real hard, someone will 'hear' me.

"Base to mobile one. Chief, we got 'em... over"

"Where is the car? Over." Chief O'Brien shouts so loud I wonder if he even needs a walkie talkie.

"Parking...over" The little black box crackles with static.

"Parking? Where is he parking? Over." The Chief sounds a little angry.

"At the carnival. Hold on for a second. They're leaving the car and walking into the carnival. Officer Lester is following. She's in street clothes...over."

"Thanks...over and out." Chief O'Brien looks around toward the main entrance. "There." He points at a man and a woman walking toward us. They're easy to see because most of the people have left the carnival already.

Tree starts to run toward his sister. "Stop!" Dad puts up his hand like a policeman stopping a car. "Tree, let's just wait and see what happens. See that woman with the baseball cap behind them? That's Officer Lester. There's no where for them to go."

It occurs to me that we are all standing in the shadows next to the trailer, while the Henderson's are in the bright lights of the carnival, which means we can see them, but they can't see us–yet. Suddenly, the couple stops. Officer Lester is so close that she almost knocks them down. She says something but keeps walking.

"Chief, I'm going to swing around to the right and get behind them," Detective Jenkins says.

"What happened?" Tree whispers.

"The officer trailing them got a little close and when they stopped, she had to keep going or else she would draw attention to herself."

"Charlie, I'm going to sneak around to the left," Dad says.

"Hank, you going to do no such thing." Mom grabs his arm.

I don't think she wants Dad to get hurt if something bad happens. Anyway, Detective Jenkins is already behind the Henderson's, who seem to be arguing about something. They're too far away for me to hear what they are saying. In less than a second, well maybe two seconds, Amelia turns away from her former husband and starts to run toward the trailer and us. Before Mr. Henderson can take a step both Detective Jenkins and Patrolman Lester grab him and pull his arms behind his back.

"Amelia!" Tree screams and runs toward his sister.

"I'm okay," she says when they reach each other. Amelia puts her arms around her brother and rests her chin on the top of his head. "I'm okay. Just a little tired."

"Good evening Amelia, my name is Hank Charles and we've been looking for you all evening."

CHAPTER TWENTY ONE
Back at Last

"I know it was dumb, but I wanted to help." Amelia starts to cry.

Tree continues to hug his sister as Dad asks, "What was dumb?"

Suddenly, Mr. Henderson screams, "Amelia, I'm warning you!"

Chief O'Brien calmly walks over to the two officers who are restraining Amelia's former husband and says, "Sir, if you utter one more threat, I will personally find some duct tape and place it over your mouth–very tightly."

Wow! The Chief was so cool. He sounded a lot like Dirty Harry. Don't be surprised, I've watched several Clint Eastwood movies.

Dad looks from Amelia to Mr. Henderson and then back to Amelia. "It's been a long night for all of us, but we need you to tell us what happened."

"It's kind of a long story," Amelia starts.

"I've given them quite a bit of background," Tree says. "I think you should start when you received that package. No doubt from him." Tree nods toward Mr. Henderson.

Everyone moves a little closer to Amelia, including Mr. Henderson, who is still being restrained by the two officers.

"Thomas found a group of people who would lend him money so that he could buy the carnival, but Tree told him that the carnival wasn't for sale," Amelia begins.

"Little fool," Mr. Henderson shouts.

"Anyway..." Amelia continues, "Thomas shows up at the carnival last week. Doesn't say a thing. He just walks around. When I got back to my trailer later in the day to get ready for a performance, I noticed that the cage door to one of my snakes was open. I thought it was strange since the snake was a water moccasin which is very, very poisonous except that I had the snake's fangs removed so that it wasn't dangerous. I don't think he knew that."

"Why do you say that?" Veronica asks.

"Because he put it under my pillow. I

assume he was trying to scare me or even worse, kill me," Amelia answers. "See, it was me, more than Tree who wanted to keep the carnival. I loved it and missed it a lot when I was gone."

This is getting creepier and creepier.

"Excuse me," the Chief says, "did you tell anyone about the snake?"

"No, who could I tell? I didn't want to upset Tree. He has so much to do every day; setting up the carnival, making sure everything is okay, breaking down the show, moving to another place. It's like three fulltime jobs. Also, I had an idea."

"Amelia, may I ask you a question?" Mom is very polite. Amelia nods. "How did you know that your former husband was responsible for putting the snake on your bed?"

"Oh! Very simple. He's so careless. When he got into my trailer, he needed to find the right cage, but he didn't want to turn on the lights because someone might see him. So he used his cigarette lighter like a flash light, only he put it down and forgot to take it with him."

"Can I ask a question, too?" Veronica has got something on her mind. "How did you know it was Mr. Henderson's cigarette lighter. Don't they all look the same?"

An excellent question. How did Amelia know?

"Most lighters look the same, except for expensive gift lighters. I gave it to him, on our fifth anniversary and had it engraved with his initials and mine."

"Do you still have the lighter?" Dad asks.

"Yes." Amelia opens her pocketbook, pushes a few things around and pulls out a shiny, almost square looking object.

"Hey, that's mine! Give it to me." Mr. Henderson demands.

"Where you are going, I don't think you'll need it," Chief O'Brien replies.

"I think you should continue," Dad suggests.

We need to find out what was in the box. Yip!

"What is it baby dog?" I wish Veronica wouldn't call me 'baby dog', especially when we're trying to investigate something important. I've got to think of a way to make her understand. It's so frustrating when you've got something to say, but can't find the words or in my case, can't speak the words. I know where to find them. I've got an idea. I walk two steps toward Mom, turn right walk two steps toward the Chief, turn right...

"The box!" Detective Jenkins pumps his fist in the air.

Yip!

"You mean the dog talks?" Amelia seems surprised.

"Sis," Tree starts, "the dog talks. Only not everyone can understand him." Amelia looks around in disbelief. First the twins nod, then Mom and Dad, then the Chief and finally Detective Jenkins. She looks at me and smiles. I sneeze in response.

"He'd make an excellent act," Amelia says.

"He also makes an excellent canine detective," the Chief responds. "...and I don't think Upton is ready to join the carnival just yet."

Yip! Thanks Chief.

DON'T TREAD ON ME

CHAPTER TWENTY TWO
Warning

Dad clears his throat. "Amelia...the box."

"Sorry. I found a box in front of my trailer two...no three days ago. It didn't have any return address on the package, only my name. I thought it was strange at first, until I opened it. Inside was a snake. A harmless common garter snake with a note saying 'Don't Tread on Me' and signed Thomas Henderson."

"The slogan 'Don't Tread on Me' was used on a flag during the American Revolution," Alex offers.

"It was a rattlesnake, I think," Veronica adds.

"Very good kids," Dad says. "The flag was called the Gadsden flag and featured a red rattlesnake on a yellow flag with the words 'Don't Tread on Me' on the bottom. It was a warning to the British of the American resolve to gain freedom."

"Hank, why a rattlesnake?" Chief O'Brien asks.

"I know...I know." Alex jumps up and down.

"Me, too." Veronica adds.

"Okay Alex, you start," Mom says.

"Rattlesnakes don't live in England, they live in America and they are very dangerous."

No kidding. All snakes, even the so-called harmless common garter snake are dangerous as far as I am concerned.

"And it was Benjamin Franklin who first came up with the idea of using the snake as a symbol of American independence," Veronica continues.

The twins have been paying attention in school. I think Benjamin Franklin did just about everything. I'd like to learn more about him, but first I'd like to get to the bottom of the missing snakes–soon.

"Please continue Amelia." Dad says.

"I was very scared. Thomas can be very dangerous. First the missing snake, then the lighter, him stalking around and of course the offer to buy the carnival. When I got the box with the note I decided I had better disappear for a while until I figured out what to do. I was pretty sure Tree wasn't going to sign the sales contract, so I thought I had a couple of days. I had to make it appear I was really leaving, so I packed up everything. I had run out on Tree once before when I married Thomas, so maybe he thought that I might be doing it again. I just needed a little time." Amelia begins to cry and once again her brother wraps his arms around her.

"Why would Mr. Henderson go to such extremes to buy the carnival?"

Another great question, Mom. It sounds like running the carnival is a lot of hard work and from what I've heard, Mr. Henderson isn't a hard worker.

"Maybe Mr. Henderson wants to give us the answer." The Chief turns toward the man being held by the Detective Jenkins and Officer Lester. "You don't have to talk. You have the right to remain silent, but it may make things easier...a lot easier if you tell us the truth about what's going on."

Mr. Henderson looks down at the ground, then at his former wife, then at the ground again.

"What's the point," he whispers.

"I'm sorry Mr. Henderson, I didn't hear you. Do you want to tell us or not?" The Chief speaks softly.

"Might as well. Might as well." Mr. Henderson shakes his head.

A uniformed policeman joins Officer

Lester and Detective Jenkins. "Need a hand?" The policeman is huge. I mean he's probably the biggest man I've ever seen. Not just tall but big like a football player.

"Thanks Biff," Detective Jenkins replies. "I think I want to tape what Mr. Henderson has to say."

"Good idea," Dad adds. "Charlie, I've got a feeling about this. I want to make sure that Mr. Henderson is aware that he doesn't have to say anything to us."

The Chief reaches into his shirt pocket and pulls out a card and begins to read. "Mr. Henderson, I want you to understand that..."

"Yeh...yeh. I know I don't have to say anything, but I might as well. Everything is ruined anyway." Mr. Henderson is still looking at the ground.

"Ready, Chief," Detective Jenkins announces. He is holding a black box. He puts a small thing in his ear and clips another small thing onto Mr. Henderson's shirt. "Mr. Henderson, I want to check for microphone volume. Please say your name so that I can make sure that the recording is clear and loud enough."

"Thomas Henderson." Mr. Henderson's voice is still almost whisper-like.

Detective Jenkins adjusts something. "Again, please."

"Thomas Henderson."

"We're good to go, Chief."

"Hank, do you want to start?" The Chief asks and Dad nods.

CHAPTER TWENTY THREE
Coming Clean

"Please state your name and address," Dad begins.

"Thomas Henderson. I don't really have an address anymore," he replies.

"Mr. Henderson, were you married to Amelia Sosolovski?" Dad continues.

"Yeh, we were married, but it didn't work." Mr. Henderson quickly looks up at his former wife, then back to the ground.

"Mr. Henderson, are you aware that you

are not required to say anything, answer our questions or tell us more than you have already done without a lawyer?" I guess Dad and the Chief want to make absolutely sure that Mr. Henderson understands his right to remain silent.

"Like I said, I know my rights. I just want to clear the air." Mr. Henderson's voice is sounder stronger. "I was really stupid. I thought that I could slide through life and not have to work like a dog...like Tree does. Only I got greedy and dumb. I wasn't satisfied with hanging around the carnival, traveling with the show, I had to steal from the people who fed me and gave me a place to live. And then Amelia kicked me out. I didn't know how to do anything and I got in trouble. I blamed Tree instead of myself. Some guys I met suggested we buy the carnival and then I could fire Tree. I never thought about the deal except to get rid of Tree and maybe get Amelia back. If Tree decided to sell the carnival, he'd retire, so I couldn't fire him. But it didn't make any difference because he wasn't going to sell. I started to hang around the carnival and I came up with the idea of trying to get to Tree by scaring Amelia. That didn't work either. She found me and told me that I was getting into trouble bigger than I could ever imagine. I didn't know what she was talking about...until tonight." Mr. Henderson looks like he's going to start crying.

"Amelia," Dad says, "could you tell us what Mr. Henderson is talking about?"

"It's simple actually. I figured that Thomas

was somehow behind the offer to purchase the carnival, but I wasn't sure why. It's a lot of work and not a lot of money. The reason Tree and I have done it all these years is because...well it's all we've ever done. Thomas was so blinded by his anger that he didn't see the forest through the trees." Amelia starts to laugh.

"It's an old family joke," her brother adds.

It's kind of a dumb joke, but since everyone else is smiling, I guess it succeeded. A joke is supposed to make people feel better—smile or laugh, even if it's dumb.

"What didn't he see?" Alex asks.

"Well, I started to ask around. The people in the carnival business, despite being competitors are very close. Almost family. I found out that the group Thomas had gotten mixed up with had tried to buy a couple of other carnivals. It didn't make sense until someone told me that the only reason these guys wanted a carnival was to hide money—illegal money. When people come to a carnival they usually pay for everything in cash—no credit cards. These people wanted to mix their illegal cash with the money we get from admissions, rides and food concessions, hoping that the police wouldn't be able to figure it out. I explained to Thomas that he was being used and that his anger should be with himself for being lazy rather than jealous of hard working people like Tree. It took a while, but I believe that Thomas now realizes how wrong he has been." Amelia walks over to her former husband and gives him a kiss on his cheek. "You're not a bad man, Thomas and I hope to take responsibility for yourself and others.

Looking up, Mr. Henderson says, "Chief, I will do everything I can to help you. Amelia... Tree, I'm so sorry."

"Mr. Henderson," the Chief begins. "Cooperating with our investigation into these people will very much be appreciated and will make it a lot easier for me to recommend leniency when the time comes, provided that neither your former wife nor your former brother-in-law wish to file a complaint against you."

"What does leniency mean?" I thought Veronica had fallen asleep. She'd been so quiet.

"It means that Mr. Henderson may not have to go to jail if he helps the Chief," Mom says. "People make mistakes and sometimes they get another chance if they take responsibility for actions."

A church bell starts to ring in the distance. Six...seven...eight...nine...ten...eleven. No wonder I'm exhausted. I can't help myself. I yawn. So does Alex, Veronica, Mom and finally Dad, who says, "It's been a long day. Time to get the Charles family home."

"Thanks for all your help—all of you." Chief O'Brien leans over and scratches my ear.

"Please be our guests at the carnival tomorrow," Tree says. "And twins, bring your friends. It's all free."

"Awesome!" The twins reply in unison.

I think I'll sleep in. One night at the carnival is quite enough for me.

The Adventures of Upton Charles
by D.G. Stern
Illustrated by Deborah Allison

Disappearing Diamonds
Something Fishy
Winter Wonderland
Lost Loot
Ship Shape

Other Books by
D.G. Stern & Deborah Allison

The Loneliest Tree

Other Books by Deborah Allison

The Lizard and The Dragonfly

Other Books by D.G. Stern

Hot Tea...Cold Case
There's Always Tomorrow
25 Days of a Tropical Christmas

Upton Charles Dog Detective

Picture Perfect

By D.G. Stern

Illustrated By
Deborah Allison

Fire engines race to a smoky house fire while Upton is on a walk with his "human" father. They are naturally drawn to the scene where they find that the home's thermostat had been turned all the way up, despite the heat of a summer day.

Inside the house the priceless collection of art is cover with soot from the smoke. Something is wrong and Upton, joined by his assistant Watson and the rest of the Charles family, intend to find the answer.

Visit Upton on the web at:
www.uptoncharles.com

ation can be obtained
ing.com
A
322
B/169

9 780990 610328